Jake Digs a Hole

by Dina Anastasio
illustrated by Lyn Boyer

Luke and the Bug Man

by Amanda Jenkins
illustrated by Shawn Byous

TWO REALISTIC FICTION STORIES

Table of Contents

Realistic Fiction

What is realistic fiction?

Realistic fiction features characters and plots that could actually happen in everyday life. The settings are authentic—they are based on familiar places such as a home, school, office, or farm. The stories involve some type of conflict, or problem. The conflict can be something a character faces within himself, an issue between characters, or a problem between a character and nature.

What is the purpose of realistic fiction?

Realistic fiction shows how people grow and learn, deal with successes and failures, make decisions, build relationships, and solve problems. In addition to making readers think and wonder, realistic fiction is entertaining. Most of us enjoy "escaping" into someone else's life for a while.

How do you read realistic fiction?

First, note the title. The title will give you a clue about an important character or conflict in the story. As you read, pay attention to the thoughts, feelings, and actions of the main characters. Note how the characters change from the beginning of the story to the end. Ask yourself: *What moves this character to action? Can I learn something from his or her struggles?*

Features of Realistic Fiction

The story takes place in an authentic setting.

At least one character deals with a conflict (self, others, or nature).

The characters are like people you might meet in real life.

The story is told from a first-person or third-person point of view.

Who tells the story in realistic fiction?

Authors usually write realistic fiction in one of two ways. In the first-person point of view, one of the characters tells the story as it happens to him or her, using words such as **I**, **me**, **my**, **mine**, **we**, **us**, and **our**. In the third-person point of view, a narrator tells the story, using words such as **he**, **she**, **they**, **their**, and the proper names of the characters.

Tools for Readers and Writers

Similes

A simile (SIH-mih-lee) is a type of figurative language in which two things are compared to each other, usually with the words **like** or **as**. For instance, "The model's pearly white smile shone like diamonds." By using **like** or **as**, similes allow both ideas to remain separate even though they are similar. Writers use similes to describe how people and ideas look and act. They also use similes to compare places to familiar objects and animals. Similes help readers create vivid images in their minds to better understand what they read.

Suffixes

Good writers use as few words as possible to convey meaning. One way they accomplish this task is by using suffixes. When suffixes are placed at the end of a root or base word, the meaning of that root word changes. For example, the Greek suffix **-ology** means "science of" or "the study of." And **-ous** means "full of." Instead of saying **the study of fossils**, writers say **paleontology**, and instead of saying **full of nerves**, writers say **nervous**.

Author's Purpose

Authors write for different reasons, or purposes, including to entertain, to persuade, and to inform. Sometimes a book is written with one purpose in mind. Other times, authors write books with many purposes. Fiction stories are usually written for entertainment purposes. But what about the author's purpose for including certain sections in her stories? These purposes include events that build the plot and develop characters. A fiction author may also have a purpose for organizing events in a certain way. While reading a story, ask questions such as, *Why did the author include that piece of information?* or *Will that piece of information help me understand a character better?*

Meet the Characters

Cave Adventures

Summer has finally arrived. Linda and her brother Jake have been coming to the same cabin on this rocky beach since they were little. Their friend Maria is back for her second summer. Cai is new to the seacoast. This summer promises new adventures since Linda and Jake's dad recently discovered a hidden cave.

Linda is a big talker with big ideas. She loves technology and gadgets, and hates that the cabins do not get TV reception or the Internet.

Jake is a smart boy who enjoys playing tricks and shooting hoops in the basket outside the cabin.

Maria is an only child. She lives with her divorced mother. She likes to bake and cook, and usually has her nose in a book.

Cai is spending the summer with his grandma. He likes to swim, fish, and play with his dog Tucker.

Oak Street Kids

Five kids couldn't be more different than Jalissa, Jamal, Brooke, Luke, and Tia. But they have some things in common, too! They all live in the Oak Street Apartments. They all have parents who work during the day. They are in the same after-school "club" run by the manager of the apartment building, Ms. Tilly. That's why the Oak Street Kids have made a deal: They will always stick together and help one another.

Jalissa likes drama and excitement, and is Jamal's twin sister.

Jamal is calm and easygoing, the opposite of his twin sister.

Brooke can always be counted on to organize and take charge.

Luke may not be a top student, but he's loyal and fun.

Tia loves every kind of sport.

Ms. Tilly is the no-nonsense manager of the Oak Street Apartments and takes care of the kids after school.

About the Settings

Cave Adventures

Dina Anastasio:
When I was a child, my sister, cousins, and I spent our summers at my grandparents' cabin on a lake. We spent our days

jumping off the end of the dock, swimming out to the raft, and exploring mysterious places with friends from other cabins.

A few years ago I discovered a place in Camden, Maine, that brought back fond memories of my grandparents' cabin. I have gone back to these cabins on the seacoast often, in part because it makes me feel connected to the "home away from home" I loved so much. There is no dock or raft to swim to, but there are caves to explore, and many of the same families return every summer. These caves, located near the water, served as the inspiration for the setting of the Cave Adventures stories.

Oak Street Kids

Amanda Jenkins: Like the Oak Street Kids characters, I lived in a garden apartment growing up in Fort Worth, Texas. There were good things and bad things about it. One bad thing was that I wasn't supposed to run and jump inside. Our apartment was upstairs, so our floor was someone else's ceiling!

One of the best things was that all kinds of kids lived there. Somebody was always playing outside, so I could just run out and join in. We played in courtyards and on patios, under stairs and along sidewalks.

Jake Digs a Hole

It was two days before the Fourth of July clambake and I was hanging out in the cave with my sister, Linda, and my friends Cai and Maria. Cai's dog, Tucker, was over by the entrance, barking at something we couldn't see.

"Looks like my mother and I will be baking all day tomorrow," Maria said. "Everybody's been asking for those little ginger cookies we make every year for the clambake, and they want our **delicious** chocolate chip brownies, too."

"You going out on old Bob's lobster boat?" Linda asked Cai. "I heard he said you're the best worker on the beach."

Cai just shrugged. He didn't say much because sometimes he was as shy as those sand crabs that Tucker liked to chase. But I could tell by the way he sort of smiled that he was flattered by what old Bob had said.

Linda did not share Cai's shyness about her own job. She'd been blabbering about it nonstop.

"*Everybody* wants my help digging for clams," she said now. "I'm the best clammer on the planet. Maybe they'll make me grand clam leader."

Rah. Rah. Rah.

I went over to the cave entrance. Tucker was still barking and yapping like a crazy hyena, so I pretended I was trying to figure out what he found so fascinating. I didn't really care what he was barking at. I just wanted to be away from that conversation.

The truth is that no one had asked me to do anything for the July Fourth clambake.

After a while Tucker's barking began to annoy me as much as their conversation, so I went home, made myself a peanut butter and banana sandwich, and took it up to my room. I put on my headphones and lay down on my bed. I must have fallen asleep because my two-hour playlist was finished when Dad knocked on my door.

"We're leaving for town in about an hour," he said. "Dress for dinner."

I put on some random going-out-to-dinner clothes and went down to the beach. I leaned against the big rock near the cave and treated myself to a **psychology** session. I felt like an earthquake in mid-eruption. My emotions were spewing all over the place. How come nobody had asked *me* to help with the clambake? Didn't anyone think I could do anything right? Was I such a loser? Did everybody think I'd mess up? Maybe they were right. If only I could think of some way to prove I wasn't a screw-up.

Cai and Tucker came by. "Why don't you come lobstering with old Bob and me tomorrow?" he asked.

Cai's a good friend, so I guess he could tell I was bummed. Don't get me wrong. It wasn't that I didn't appreciate what he was trying to do, but I needed to figure this out by myself. I'd decided to do something so special that everyone would gasp and say, "Jake is as brilliant as Einstein! Why didn't we know this before? Is it possible we weren't paying attention?" So I changed the subject.

"What time do the fireworks happen on the Fourth?" I asked.

"I think the clambake begins at 5:00 or 5:30, and when it starts to get dark we all head into town to watch the fireworks."

My father was calling me. "Ready, Jake? It's 4:00. Time to go." It sure was—Cai and I were ankle-deep in the water from the incoming tide.

The next day was awfully boring. Everybody was baking or making potato salad or down at the supermarket buying napkins and paper cups and other stuff for the clambake. I shot hoops and spent some time playing games on various gadgets. At 3:00 I went down to the cave to see if anybody was around, but the cave was empty. Cai and Maria like it that way, but the place makes me lonely when I'm by myself, so I beat it out of there.

Linda was leaning against the big rock. Her bucket was a few feet away, which meant she was waiting for Mom so they could go clamming.

"Want to come with us?" Linda asked.

"No thanks." I found a stick and drew a picture of an elephant in the sand. I was adding an upside-down trunk when Linda said she'd forgotten something and went up to the cabin.

She'd been gone about a minute when I decided to fill her bucket with sand. I have no idea why I did it. Later I realized it was a childish thing to do, but it seemed like a good idea at the time, so I dropped the stick and kept scooping up handfuls of sand until it was full.

Linda came back a few minutes later. When she noticed that her bucket was full of sand she just looked at me like I was crazy and said, "Why do you always do stuff like that?"

"I have no idea," I said, which was the truth.

She shook her head and looked at her watch. "It's 4:00. Time to go clamming with Mom. How about an **apology** for being so thoughtless?"

"Sorry," I said.

She dumped out the sand, rinsed the bucket, and went back to our cabin.

Old Bob came by a few minutes later. "Seen Cai?" he asked. I shook my head.

"Mind telling him to meet me tomorrow morning at 10:00? He knows, but just remind him."

"I'll tell him," I said.

I forgot all about telling Cai until almost 10:00 the next morning, when I looked out my window and saw him running down toward old Bob's boat. For some reason it annoyed me that Cai had remembered and I hadn't.

It was July Fourth and the beach was crowded despite the overcast skies. Everybody was staring up at the gray clouds wondering if a monsoon was going to obliterate the clambake. I settled down on the porch and watched the proceedings.

The cave seemed to be the official clambake headquarters. People were going in with wicker baskets and paper bags and plastic containers filled with all sorts of salads and corn on the cob wrapped in tinfoil.

The weather was gloomy and depressing, like my mood. It rained off and on, but nobody pulled the plug on the clambake.

I wanted to be part of it, but not in a hanging-out-on-the-beach kind of way. I needed to do something special. Something that would prove I wasn't a loser. But what?

Bob's boat came in at about 1:00. A few minutes later, Linda carried two buckets of clams into the cave.

At 3:00 the rain stopped and the sun came out. An older town kid named Ralph was digging the clambake pit next to the big rock by the cave. When he was finished, he started carrying rocks to the hole and placing them inside.

As I watched him, my mind went into overdrive. There was something wrong with what he was doing. Finally, it hit me!

I needed to confirm my hunch so I went inside and examined the chart on the kitchen wall. Just as I suspected! I went back outside thinking I could make a big scene and get credit for saving the day. But that would make Ralph look bad. So I decided to be a nice guy. I went down to the rock and pointed at the pit.

"You're going to be sorry you dug that hole there. It won't be long before your pit looks like an **enormous** bucket of soup."

"Get lost," Ralph snarled, without even looking at me. Ralph turned out to be not as nice a guy as I was!

"Have it your way," I said. I went and got a shovel from the shed and started digging a hole higher up the beach, closer to the cabins.

"How's the hole coming, Jake?" Ralph hollered in an **obnoxious** voice every five minutes or so.

There were lots of people around and some of them laughed, but I didn't care. I was on a mission.

I was searching for rocks when old Bob came by. He stared into my pit for a while, and then he strolled down to the big rock. I went with him.

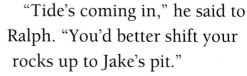

"Tide's coming in," he said to Ralph. "You'd better shift your rocks up to Jake's pit."

Everybody stopped what they were doing and noticed what I'd figured out earlier. The tide was rising, and it wasn't going to stop before it reached Ralph's pit.

"Why didn't you just say so?" Ralph said, looking at me now.

"I tried to tell you," I insisted, "but you wouldn't listen."

There were high fives and comments about how brilliant I'd been to pay attention to the tide, after which we moved the rocks up to my pit, covered them with wood and seaweed, and got the fire started.

We had a couple of hours before the fire would be ready for cooking, so Cai and I went down to the cave. It was as crowded as my school gym when we were in the basketball finals.

"I don't like this," Cai muttered. "It's *our* private cave."

"It will be again," I said.

"Maybe," Cai grumbled. Then he asked, "What made you think about high tide?"

"Two days ago the water at the big rock was up to my ankles at 4:00. Yesterday at 4:00 I was in the same exact spot as the **previous** day and my feet were dry. I was even drawing in the sand. According to the tide chart on my wall, today's high tide will happen at about 5:16, just in time for the clambake."

Cai patted me on the back. "You saved the day."

"I guess I did!" I said, suddenly excited about the clambake after all.

Analyze the Characters, Setting, and Plot

- What is the setting for this story?
- Who are the main characters in this story?
- What is the problem in this story?
- Describe Jake.
- Jake doesn't want to go clamming with Cai. Why not?
- What does Jake figure out?
- How does Jake solve his problem?
- How does the story end?

Focus on Comprehension: Author's Purpose

- What is the author's purpose for writing this realistic fiction story?
- For what purpose does the author include the incident where Jake fills Linda's bucket with sand?
- The author says that Ralph told Jake to get lost when Jake told him about the problem with his clambake hole. Why did the author have Ralph react in this manner?

Analyze the Tools Writers Use: Simile

Locate the following similes in the story and answer the questions.
- On page 9, Jake compares Tucker with a crazy hyena. What is the author trying to tell you? Explain.
- On page 9, Jake says that he felt like an earthquake in mid-eruption. Does this simile describe calmness or anger? Explain.
- On page 12, Jake compares his mood to weather. How is this a simile?
- On page 13, Jake tells Ralph that his pit will look like an enormous bucket of soup. What is Jake implying with this simile?

Focus on Words: Suffixes

Make a chart like the one below. For each word, identify its part of speech. Then identify the base or root word and suffix. Finally, identify the word's meaning.

Page	Word	Part of Speech	Base or Root Word	Suffix	Definition
8	delicious				
9	psychology				
11	apology				
13	enormous				
14	obnoxious				
15	previous				

Luke and the Bug Man

Brooke, Jamal, Jalissa, and Tia huddled on the sidewalk after school, anxiously waiting for their friend Luke. Today, notice-of-failure reports had gone out to kids who were in danger of flunking a class. Luke usually got a notice-of-failure report, and he was always depressed and upset afterward.

The school's double doors flew open and Luke burst out. "*Yahoo!*" he shouted, bounding down the steps.

"You're not failing anything!" Tia said in delight.

"Of course I am!" Luke said cheerfully. "I'm failing science! I got a zero on a major assignment. See, I accidentally left it wadded up in my pocket and it went through the washing machine. I found it a couple of days later and turned it in, but Ms. Zamboni said that with all the ink washed off, it didn't demonstrate any knowledge of biology. I tried to get partial credit for explaining about the power of the rinse cycle, but she didn't go for it."

"So why are you happy?" asked Jamal.

"You know how the Bug Man's coming tomorrow?"

The others nodded. The Bug Man was a TV personality with an educational show about insects. He was going to present a program to the entire school the next morning. Luke, a huge fan of the Bug Man, had been ecstatic ever since the presentation was announced.

Now Luke was so excited that he was bouncing on his toes. "Ms. Zamboni's giving me extra credit to stay late and help the Bug Man set up this afternoon! That means I could actually get a *B* in science! *Me*—a *B*! Can you believe it? *Woo-hoo*!" Luke pumped his fists into the air like a football player who's just won the championship game.

The author's use of an easy-to-visualize simile helps bring Luke's enthusiasm alive for the reader.

"We'll stay and help, too," Jamal told Luke.

"Yes!" Jalissa said. "We'll help you get that extra credit!"

After calling Ms. Tilly to let her know they'd be late, Jalissa, Jamal, Brooke, and Tia settled on the steps to wait for the Bug Man. Luke paced back and forth. "I can't wait to meet the Bug Man in person!" he said. "I know his scientific words are boring, and he's nerdy-looking and dresses like a total geek—but I *love* the gross stuff on his show! Last week he showed a close-up of a praying mantis eating a lizard!"

"*Blech*!" shrieked Jalissa. "That's disgusting!"

Another way to tell that this is realistic fiction is that Luke and his friends act like kids you might meet in real life—or already know.

As she spoke, a van pulled up to the curb. It was painted to look like a dragonfly and had huge iridescent wings attached to the roof.

"It's the Bugmobile!" Luke said in an awed voice. "He's here!"

The Bug Man was a large man in a polka-dot bow tie. His pants were so short that the kids could see his argyle socks.

He got out of his van sipping from a can of lemonade and holding a half-eaten caramel apple. He polished off the caramel apple, set his drink on the curb, and opened the back door of the van.

Luke rushed over. "We're official volunteers, here to help you set up!"

The Bug Man peered at Luke through thick-lensed glasses, then studied the other kids. "Very well. Four of you can get that big folding table out of my van." He picked up a large insect cage and headed toward the school. "And one of you can open the door for me."

In the dialogue that follows, the author gives Luke another problem, stemming from his enthusiastic personality: His inability to control his excitement gets him into trouble with his idol.

"I'll do it!" Luke raced ahead, flung the door open, and stood at attention like a sentry. "*Beep! Beep!* Look out!" he shouted as the Bug Man maneuvered his cage through the doorway. "Wide load, coming through!"

The Bug Man stopped short, offended. "I beg your pardon!"

"Oh!" Luke said, "I didn't mean you, sir. I totally forgot that you're . . ."

The Bug Man frowned at Luke as if he were an especially unpleasant cockroach.

"R-really," Luke stammered, "I don't care that you're um . . . big. Just like I don't care that your big words are boring."

"Oh?" boomed the Bug Man. "You consider my use of proper **terminology** to be **tedious**? **Monotonous**? Uninspiring?"

"No, just plain old boring," said Luke. "Oh. No, wait. Mr. Bug, I mean, Mr. Man—"

"My name is Cyrus Poppermill," said the Bug Man. "*Doctor* Poppermill; I have a Ph.D. in

entomology. Go away, please. With four other helpers, I certainly don't need *you*." He hefted the cage a little higher and disappeared down the hall.

Luke's shoulders slumped. Like a puppy with its tail between its legs, he slunk back to Jalissa, Brooke, Tia, and Jamal, who were carefully easing a long table out of the van.

Luke groaned and sat on the curb. "The Bug Man fired me!" he informed the others, "even though I'm a volunteer!"

"Already?" Jalissa wailed. "What happened?"

"I don't know! I was trying to be nice, but somehow everything came out wrong."

"Maybe he'll give you another chance," said Jamal.

Luke shook his head. "The Bug Man hates me." He stared glumly at the Bug Man's open can of lemonade. "I've got to tell him I'm sorry, though. I think I hurt his feelings."

"If you apologize, he might re-hire you as a volunteer," Brooke pointed out.

"You think so?" Luke looked hopeful. "Hey, you're right!" He jumped up, accidentally knocking over the can. "Rats!" he cried, snatching at it.

A yellow-and-black insect flew out of the opening and into Luke's face.

"Augh! Ouch!" Luke jumped back, dancing around and slapping at the air.

The author introduces a plot point.

"A bee's attacking Luke!" shouted Jalissa.

The last of the Bug Man's lemonade seeped into the ground as the other kids gathered around Luke. The insect had already disappeared, but four red welts were rising on Luke's mouth.

The author adds a plot twist and brings it to life with humorous dialogue.

"At least you're not allergic to stings," Brooke tried to console him.

Luke nodded dismally. "I ged stug aw de tibe," he agreed, then, "*ow!* It huts to tawk."

"What did he say?" Tia asked. Brooke and Jalissa shrugged, mystified.

"He said, 'I get stung all the time,'" Jamal told them. "And 'It hurts to talk.'"

"Dish ish teddible!" said Luke, wincing.

"'This is terrible,'" Jamal translated.

"How cad I . . . *ow!*"

"'How can I,'" said Jamal.

". . . apowogize to de Bug Bad . . . *ow!*"

"'Apologize to the Bug Man,'" said Jamal.

". . . wid a shtug wip?" Luke finished in despair.

"'With a stung lip,'" Jamal whispered sadly.

Brooke patted Luke's arm. "Don't give up! I'll get you a notepad and pencil out of my backpack. You can write your apology down and hand it to the Bug Man."

She had just given Luke the pad and pencil when Cyrus Poppermill came out. He looked displeased to see Luke but said nothing as he waddled toward the van.

Writing was a lot slower than talking. Luke could have blurted out an entire sentence in the time it took just to set the tip of the pencil on the paper.

It's okay with me that you're overweight, Luke started to write—but then he remembered that was offensive. He thought a moment and then wrote: I'M SORRY I WAS RUDE. I DIDN'T MEAN TO BE.

The author uses the plot point about Luke's bee sting to develop the story and show Luke learning something about himself. Characters who show growth are often more appealing.

He showed the note to Cyrus Poppermill. Cyrus looked slightly less displeased.

I really don't mind the boring parts of your show, Luke thought. But he reconsidered, and wrote: I'M YOUR BIGGEST FAN. I'D NEVER WANT TO HURT YOUR FEELINGS.

Cyrus read the note, and his disapproving expression faded.

I don't even care that you're a nerdy-looking geek, Luke thought. But what he ended up writing was: PLEASE GIVE ME ANOTHER CHANCE.

"Well," Cyrus Poppermill conceded, "perhaps you were simply overly excited. I suppose you may continue your assistance."

Luke didn't smile—that would have hurt—but he was overjoyed. He decided he'd try more often to slow down and think before he spoke.

"Are those insect bites on your lip?" Cyrus asked Luke.

Luke nodded. I GOT STUNG BY A BEE, he wrote.

"A bee?" Cyrus read, **incredulous**. "One *single* bee? Impossible! Insects of the genus *Apis* sting once, leave their stingers behind, and die immediately afterward. Was there a stinger left in your face?"

Luke shook his head.

"I thought not! Your injury was probably perpetrated by a member of genus *Vespula*, which has similar coloring to *Apis* but normally leaves *no* stinger behind and can sting *multiple* times."

I DIDN'T GET A GOOD LOOK. IT WAS HIDING IN YOUR LEMONADE.

"*Aha!*" Cyrus said, triumphant. "*Vespula* is often attracted to sugary beverage containers."

"What's a *vespula*?" Tia whispered to Brooke.

VESPULA = YELLOW-JACKET WASP, wrote Luke. *APIS* = HONEYBEE.

"Whoa," said Jamal. "Looks like some of those big words sank in, Luke! You *deserve* to get that *B* in science!"

Luke looked surprised and then pleased.

"This young man certainly knows his **taxonomy**," Cyrus agreed. "And he handles his injuries with fortitude. It reminds me of the time I was bitten by a poisonous beetle with mandibles as wide as hedge clippers."

MANDIBLES = JAWS, Luke wrote, proudly explaining to the others.

"My hand turned green and putrid and swelled to the size of a football!" The Bug Man's eyes gleamed with pleasure at the memory.

Luke wrote something down and handed it to Cyrus Poppermill. THAT'S THE AWESOMEST THING I'VE EVER HEARD.

Cyrus beamed at Luke. "I can see that you're a young man who appreciates the viscerally compelling aspects of the insect world!"

"What did he just say?" asked Jamal.

"He lubs de gwose shtuff, too," Luke translated.

"I love the gross stuff, too," agreed the Bug Man.

Reread the Story

Analyze the Characters, Setting, and Plot

- Who are the main characters in this story?
- What is the problem in this story?
- List Luke's infractions against the Bug Man.
- How do Luke and the Bug Man communicate?
- How is the problem solved?
- How does the story end?

Focus on Comprehension: Author's Purpose

- What is the author's purpose for writing this realistic fiction story?
- For what purpose does the author include the back-and-forth dialogue between Luke and Jamal after Luke has been stung?
- Why does the author use capital letters every time Luke writes something down on paper?

Focus on Point of View

Point of view means the grammatical person's perspective from which a story is told. There are three points of view.

First-person point of view uses the main character as the narrator of the story. This type of story is told from the "I" point of view.

Second-person point of view uses the understood "you" as the narrator of the story. This point of view is rarely used in narratives.

Third-person point of view uses pronouns like **he**, **she**, and **it**. The narrator is not identified in the story.

From which point of view are the two stories in this book written?

Analyze the Tools Writers Use: Simile

Locate the following similes in the story and answer the questions.

- On page 20, the author compares Luke to a football player who's just won the championship game. How does this simile help you understand Luke's feelings?
- On page 22, the author says that Luke stood at the door like a sentry. How is this a simile?
- On page 22, the author compares Luke to an especially unpleasant cockroach. How is this a simile?
- On page 23 the author says that Luke slinks back to the kids like a puppy with its tail between its legs. What is the author implying with this simile?

Focus on Words: Suffixes

Make a chart like the one below. For each word, identify its part of speech. Then identify the base or root word and suffix. Finally, identify the word's meaning.

Page	Word	Part of Speech	Base or Root Word	Suffix	Definition
22	terminology				
22	tedious				
22	monotonous				
23	entomology				
26	incredulous				
27	taxonomy				

How does an author write

Realistic Fiction?

Reread "Luke and the Bug Man" and think about what Amanda Jenkins did to write this story. How did she develop it? How can you, as a writer, develop your own story?

1. Decide on a Problem

Remember, the characters in realistic fiction face the same problems you might face. In "Luke and the Bug Man" the problem is that Luke needs to help the Bug Man, a TV personality speaking at his school, in order to get extra credit so he can pass science—but he unintentionally insults the Bug Man on meeting him.

Character	Luke	Jamal	Cyrus Poppermill: the Bug Man
Traits	overeager; into bugs	helpful; sympathetic	sensitive; forgiving
Examples	is so excited to see the Bug Man he unintentionally insults him by speaking without thinking first; he knows a lot about insects, including some difficult words that describe them	offers to help Luke get his extra credit and translates for Luke when Luke's lips get stung; feels as sad as Luke does when it looks like Luke won't be able to apologize to the Bug Man	gets easily insulted by Luke without realizing that Luke is just a young, overexcited fan; forgives Luke when he's praised and also because he's impressed with Luke's knowledge of insects

Brainstorm Characters

Writers ask these questions:
- What kind of person will my main character be? What are his or her traits? Interests?
- What things are important to my main character? What does he or she want?
- What other characters will be important to my story? How will each one help or hinder the main character?
- How will the characters change? What will they learn about life?

 ## Brainstorm Setting and Plot

Writers ask these questions:
- Where does my story take place? How will I describe the setting?
- What is the problem, or situation?
- What events happen? How does the story end?
- Will my readers be entertained? Will they learn something?

Setting	the Oak Street Kids' school
Problem of the Story	Luke needs to help the Bug Man, a TV personality, set things up to speak at Luke's school in order for Luke to pass science, but he unintentionally insults the Bug Man on meeting him.
Story Events	1. Notice-of-failure reports have been given out. Jamal, Tia, Brooke, and Jalissa wait for Luke, knowing he'll get one. 2. Luke gets a notice-of-failure report for science but he can get extra credit by helping the Bug Man, a TV personality Luke admires, set up for his lecture at the school. 3. The Bug Man arrives and Luke is so excited that he unintentionally insults him and gets fired from volunteering. 4. Luke decides to apologize and see if he'll be forgiven, but an insect stings him, making him unable to talk. 5. Brooke gives Luke paper and a pencil, which allows Luke to think before he writes.
Solution to the Problem	The Bug Man accepts Luke's written apology and the two bond over their love of insects.

Glossary

apology   (uh-PAH-luh-jee) an admission of regret (page 11)

delicious   (dih-LIH-shus) very tasty (page 8)

enormous   (ih-NOR-mus) huge (page 13)

entomology   (en-tuh-MAH-luh-jee) the study of insects (page 23)

incredulous   (in-KREH-juh-lus) unbelieving (page 26)

monotonous   (muh-NAH-tuh-nus) boringly repetitive (page 22)

obnoxious   (ahb-NAHK-shus) unpleasant and irritating (page 14)

previous   (PREE-vee-us) coming before (page 15)

psychology   (sy-KAH-luh-jee) the study of the mind and behavior (page 9)

taxonomy   (tak-SAH-nuh-mee) a system of classifying animals and plants (page 27)

tedious   (TEE-dee-us) dull and tiring (page 22)

terminology   (ter-mih-NAH-luh-jee) the language used to discuss a certain field of study (page 22)